On the Loose

Suddenly the tiger and the cage started to swim before his eyes.

Waves of heat like those that rise from desert sands made his eyes water. The tiger and the cage were melting away.

Red blinked. He rubbed his eyes. He tried to focus them—and was blinded by white light exploding.

The light faded and his vision returned.

His mouth dropped open.

The cage was empty.

"Where is the—?" he started to ask himself.

A huge roar came from behind him.

A tiger's roar.

THE X FILES™

Created by Chris Carter

TIGER, TIGER

A novel by Les Martin

Based on the teleplay written
by Chris Carter, creator of the
television series, *The X-Files*.

HarperCollins
An imprint of HarperCollins *Publishers*

To Nicole,
my greatest fan and severest critic

First published in the USA in 1995 by HarperTrophy
a division of HarperCollins*Publishers*

First published in Great Britain in 1996 by
HarperCollins*Publishers* Ltd
77-85 Fulham Palace Road
Hammersmith, London W6 8JB

1 3 5 7 9 10 8 6 4 2

The X-Files ™ © 1995 by
Twentieth Century Fox Film Corporation
All rights reserved

ISBN 0 00 675184-9

Printed and bound in Great Britain
by HarperCollins Manufacturing Ltd, Glasgow

Cover photograph: Michael Grecco
Cover photograph © by Twentieth Century Fox Corporation

Chapter ONE

"Nobody is paying you to dance, Roberto," Francisco García told his nephew. He spoke in Spanish, above the Latin music from Roberto's boom box. "Remember, God is watching."

Francisco pointed to the TV camera trained on them from the ceiling of the building where they were working. The building housed the Idaho Mutual Insurance Trust. The bank was the biggest in Fairfield, Idaho, with high ceilings and gleaming marble floors. Francisco and Roberto mopped those floors each night.

Francisco had to admit that he enjoyed the sight of Roberto dancing to the radio, using his mop as a partner. The young were entitled to a little fun. But as Roberto's uncle, he had to keep the young man in line.

"You lose your job, and it's back to the jungle in El Salvador," he told Roberto sternly.

Roberto responded with a grin. He did one more fast step. Then he turned off the music and went back to work.

Satisfied, Francisco attacked a nasty stain on the floor with his squeegee.

1

Then a strange rumbling filled the air.

The marble floor trembled.

Back in El Salvador Francisco had felt earthquakes. And he had heard the sounds of war as well.

But this was Idaho. There were no earthquakes here. No wars either. This was a land of peace and plenty. But Francisco knew the sound of trouble when he heard it.

There was more rumbling, louder and closer.

Francisco's gaze darted around the bank, looking for a safe spot. The perfect place would have been the vaults. But of course the huge metal doors were locked. Perhaps behind the counter—

Before he could move, the plate glass front of the bank exploded. Instinctively Francisco shut his eyes against the splinters showering inward. He felt a stinging on his cheek. Then there was silence.

Slowly he let out his breath. He opened his eyes and touched his cheek. His fingertip gleamed with blood. But other than that scratch, he was untouched. He looked at his nephew. Roberto was safe, though shaking like a leaf. Francisco realized he was shaking too. He crossed himself.

He heard the rumbling again. It was more distant now. It was going away.

Cautiously Francisco led the way over the shards of glass glittering on the marble floor. He and Roberto reached the gaping hole that had been the window. They looked out.

"Mother of God. This cannot be happening," Francisco said.

But it was. They saw a car down the street crumpling as if hit by a gigantic sledgehammer. They saw a wooden newsstand splintering into matchsticks.

But they could not see what did it.

The force that smashed into the bank, the car, the newsstand, was invisible.

Francisco and Roberto looked at each other. Each knew what the other was thinking.

Maybe they had not been so smart to come to Idaho after all. Back at home at least they knew where danger came from. Here they were suddenly strangers—and afraid.

Ray Hines was no stranger to Idaho. He had been born and raised there. He had helped build highways across the state's vast highland plains and through its rugged mountains. Tonight he was enjoying his job. The construction company was in a hurry to finish a new four-lane highway to Fairfield. That meant overtime pay.

Hines was taking a coffee break with his fellow workers when he heard the rumbling.

He peered down the unfinished highway.

"What the devil?" he said, his mouth dropping open.

One lane of the road was lined with barricades to keep off traffic. The barricades were heavy wood, but now they were being flipped aside as if they were cardboard. One by one they tumbled over.

Something big and strong was coming down the pike.

Hines would have said a twister, but he couldn't feel a breath of wind.

He couldn't see a thing either.

Not even when it hit him—and sent him flying through the air.

Out of the corner of his eye, Hines saw his Thermos in the air as well, spraying coffee.

That was the last thing he saw.

His body hit the last stretch of highway he had laid down. The last he ever would lay down.

Ray Hines' coffee break was going to last forever.

Thirty miles down the highway, Wesley Brewer was enjoying the newly paved surface. If all roads were like this, driving his big tractor-trailer would be a cinch. Especially when he didn't have a load. He could really let her go all out. As far as Brewer was concerned, it beat flying.

It had been a long night's ride, though. Brewer yawned as he turned on his CB radio.

"This is Wesley Brewer out on Route Seven," he said. "Looking like an eight o'clock estimated arrival time on that cargo pickup."

He rubbed sleep out of his eyes as he waited for an answer.

Suddenly his eyes bulged.

Suddenly sleep was a million miles away.

Dead ahead, only a few hundred feet away, was a sight Brewer had seen before only on a circus poster.

A huge elephant.

This elephant wasn't on a poster.

It was charging up the highway straight at him.

Brewer slammed on the brakes. He prayed they would hold.

The tractor-trailer skidded. Started to spin out of control. Then came to a stop.

The elephant stopped too.

The huge machine and the huge animal faced each other, inches apart.

Brewer looked into the elephant's glinting eyes. He saw the menacing points of its long ivory tusks. He watched its gray trunk slap against his windshield.

Dimly he heard a voice on his CB. "Give me that ETA again. Brewer? Brewer, you copy?"

Brewer didn't think of answering. His hands were white-knuckled on the steering wheel. They relaxed when he saw the elephant turn. It lumbered away, tail swishing, toward the blazing rim of the rising sun. Then, as if hit by an electric prod, it broke into a run. Huge as it was, it moved startlingly fast.

Brewer watched it disappear around a bend in the road. He waited for the pounding of his heart to slow. Then he said over his CB, "I know you're not going to believe this, but—"

The sun was clear of the horizon when the police caught up with the elephant. It was easy. There was no chase.

A motorist had spotted it and reported it.

It was still lying on the highway in the same spot when the two squad cars arrived, lights blinking, sirens wailing. Other cars were already there. Men, women, and children stared at the fallen beast.

"Keep back!" a cop told the crowd. "It's still alive and dangerous."

The elephant *was* still alive. Barely.

Its flanks heaved painfully. Its trunk slapped the road feebly. It strained to rise to its feet.

Its effort seemed to exhaust it. It slumped back. It lay quivering a moment. Then it was still.

"Mommy, Mommy, it gone to sleep?" a little boy asked.

The mother bit her lip as the boy looked up at her. "Yes, dear, it's gone to sleep," she assured him.

The little boy's sister was old enough to take a step closer to the fallen elephant.

She was old enough to take a long look at it.

She was old enough to burst into tears at what she saw.

Chapter TWO

The media had fun with the story.

A radio newsman joked, "This elephant had his trunk packed but nowhere to go."

A TV anchor wisecracked, "Home, home on the range, where the deer and the elephants play."

A paper sold in supermarkets ran this headline, MOVE OVER, DUMBO! REAL LIFE FLYING ELEPHANT MAKES A CRASH LANDING!

After a quick look, the local police tried to forget it too. The trail of destruction, the elephant on the loose—none of it made any sense. The cops had plenty of cases that did. They had no time to waste on a headache like this. They buried it in their files. Out of sight, out of mind.

But the case went into another set of files as well.

The X-files.

They were files kept in a top-secret room at F.B.I. headquarters in Washington, D.C. They held reports of strange cases received from all over the country. Cases that no one could explain. Cases that even the F.B.I. would have been happy to forget.

Except for a couple of agents who would not let those cases rest.

"When's the next flight to Idaho?" Fox Mulder asked Dana Scully.

"There's a red-eye flight to Boise at three A.M.," she told him. "We can rent a car there to drive to Fairfield."

"Let's get packed, then," he said.

"I already am," Scully answered. "I knew wild elephants couldn't keep you away."

Mulder gave Scully a grin. She gave him back a half smile. She had come a long way since she'd started working with him.

At first she'd thought he was a little crazy, just as his bosses at the Bureau did.

But no longer.

She had moved a lot closer to Mulder's point of view. She had learned that crazy things could happen in the world.

And that it was really crazy to pretend that they didn't.

"Now I know where my taxes go," Stan Weitz, the Camus County sheriff, told Mulder and Scully the next day as they sat with him in his office. "Flying all this way from Washington on a wild-goose chase. Wild-elephant chase, anyway."

Mulder waited patiently for the sheriff to stop chuckling at his own joke. He wondered how many elephant jokes he would hear before this case was over. Too many, for sure.

He looked at his watch. "Well, no sense wasting government time," he said. "Let's get to work."

"Sure," the sheriff said. "I expect you want to read our official report. I'll fish it out of the files."

"We've already read it, " Mulder said. "On the plane."

"We got it out of our files," Scully explained. "It was forwarded to Bureau headquarters. Part of a computerized system we've set up in police departments all over the country. It lets us react immediately to—emergencies."

"Oh yeah, I forgot," the sheriff said. "I heard something about that from my staff techies. I gotta say, I don't hold much with all these new gadgets. Give me old-fashioned police work. Shoe leather beats computer chips every time."

"I agree," Mulder said. "Can you take us to where the trouble started?"

"Can do," the sheriff said. "But you won't find out anything more than we did. Which was nothing."

They left the Fairfield police station and got into the sheriff's squad car. The bank was a five-minute drive away. Its plate glass front still had not been repaired. Local citizens stood gawking at the gaping hole. Fairfield wasn't a town where strange things happened. A broken streetlight would have been big news here.

Two Latinos in janitors' clothes stood in front of the building. One was middle-aged, the other in his early twenties. Both looked scared.

"I told these two to show up here when you faxed me," the sheriff said. "I figured you'd want to see them. They were eyewitnesses to the . . ." the sheriff said. He paused, looking for the right word. "To the whatever-it-was" was the best he could come up with.

"I think you should question them," Mulder told Scully. "I'll check out the inside of the bank."

"Right," said Scully.

But before she began, she said to the sheriff, "Thanks a lot. We can take over from here. I'm sure you have other things to do."

"Sure do," the sheriff agreed. "Well, I wish you folks luck. You'll need it."

He got into his squad car and drove off.

Scully turned toward the two janitors. As she had hoped, they looked more relaxed now that the sheriff was gone. Police garb definitely put them on edge.

"What are your names?" she asked them.

"Francisco García, and this is my nephew Roberto," the older man answered. "Believe me, miss, we had nothing to do with the broken glass. We are good, careful workers. We never do anything wrong. We obey all the laws. We try always to be good Americans. We want to be citizens someday."

"Please, don't worry. You have nothing to fear from us," Scully assured him. "We simply want to know what you saw the night the glass window exploded."

"We saw nothing," Francisco said.

"Nothing," Roberto agreed.

"No one outside?" asked Scully.

"No," Roberto insisted. "I went to look. But I saw nothing."

"Did you hear anything?" asked Scully.

"A noise. Yes," Francisco said.

"Like thunder it was," Roberto added. "First it was loud, then it was fainter."

"Anything else?" Scully said, jotting down their remarks.

Both men shook their heads.

Scully waited to see if they'd remember anything more. They didn't.

"Thank you," she told them. "Your help is appreciated."

"You are police too?" Francisco asked.

"Yes," Scully had to admit. "From the federal government. F.B.I."

"Nothing will happen to us, please?" Francisco said.

"Nothing will happen to you," Scully told him.

"Thank you, miss, thank you," Francisco said.

The two men had learned back in El Salvador that the less you had to do with the law, the better. Now they moved away as fast as they could without seeming to run.

Meanwhile, Mulder had returned. "Nothing inside except heaps of broken glass," he said. "What did the janitors say?"

"They claim they saw nothing," Scully said. "They just heard a loud noise that they couldn't identify. I have a sense that they're telling the truth."

"They probably are," Mulder said. "The TV security cameras in the bank don't show anything either. Just a giant explosion of glass flying inward. As if from some kind of shock wave outside."

"Which leaves us with nothing to go on," Scully said, shaking her head.

"So what else is new, partner?" Mulder said. "We're in X-files land. Starting with a blank slate comes with the territory. The fun is filling the blanks in."

"Sure," said Scully. "Like working out a crossword puzzle in a language you don't understand."

"A language you have to learn to understand," Mulder told her, "if you want to get a message you can't afford to miss."

Chapter THREE

Scully glanced at her notes. "The police report said the trail of damage goes up this street," she said.

"Let's follow it," replied Mulder.

Before they started walking, Scully took one more look at the gaping hole in the glass.

"The noise the janitors described—it could have been a sonic boom," she suggested.

"Yeah, well, no sonic boom did that," said Mulder, pointing down the street to a car parked at a weird angle. Its trunk was bashed in. So was part of its side. Beyond the car, a metal street sign was twisted as if it were made of Silly Putty. "Or that either," he added.

"Or this." As they walked past it, Mulder indicated a newsstand that had been smashed to splinters.

"Right. Cross off the sonic boom theory," Scully agreed.

"Then there's this photo," he said. He handed Scully a copy of a photo that had been faxed to F.B.I. headquarters along with the police report.

Scully glanced at it to refresh her memory. It was not a pretty picture. A corpse never was.

14

"This man had his spine broken like a tooth-pick," Mulder reminded her. "And there was a bruise on his body that was roughly the size and shape of an elephant's foot. The other men working on the road said they felt the ground shake. Then they caught the faint whiff of an animal odor on the wind."

"I know what you're thinking, Mulder," Scully said. "That elephant they found dead did it all." She shook her head. "I don't buy it. It defies logic. Someone would have seen it."

"If someone saw it, we wouldn't be here, Scully," said Mulder.

He gave her a smile. Scully didn't smile back. She had her own ideas. And she used her own eyes.

She moved to check out the bashed car again. The twisted street sign. The totaled newsstand.

Mulder followed her as she made the rounds. "A vehicle would have left evidence of a collision," he told her. "There would be bits of paint. Or metallic scratches. I see no sign of either. Do you?"

Scully examined the twisted sign. She shook her head.

"I'd allow there's the outside chance of a tornado," Mulder went on. "Even though it's not tornado season. I'd even allow there's a chance that a black hole in space might have passed over the area. But . . ."

He paused and waited until Scully asked, "But what, Mulder?"

"But if I was a betting man, I'd say it was—" Mulder began.

"An invisible elephant?"

"You said it—I didn't," said Mulder.

"You didn't have to," said Scully. "I know the way your mind works."

"Do you know I once saw the magician David Copperfield make the Statue of Liberty disappear?" said Mulder. "An elephant would be child's play for someone with the right tools."

"Sure, Mulder," said Scully. "Some mad magician came to Fairfield with smoke and mirrors."

"Maybe not a magician," said Mulder. "And maybe not smoke and mirrors. But someone, something, with some kind of —"

He got no further.

A large truck pulled up to the curb near them.

Painted on the side of the truck were the silhouette of a leaping tiger and the words FAIRFIELD ZOO.

The driver's door opened and a man in a green zoo attendant's uniform got out. His hair was graying and thinning, and his stomach hung over his belt. But there were strength and swagger in his stride as he came over to the two agents.

"Agent Mulder?" he asked.

"Yes," Mulder said.

"I'm Ed Meecham, Fairfield Zoo. I got your fax to meet you. I checked with the sheriff and he told me you'd be here. Sorry if I'm a little late, but we had some trouble transporting Ganesha's body this morning."

"This is Agent Scully," Mulder said. Meecham nodded, as if he was noticing her for the first time. Funny how some people simply couldn't see a woman as an F.B.I. agent, Mulder thought. Even one as sharp-looking as Scully. They had to keep being told.

"Hi," Meecham said, and started to turn back to Mulder.

Before he could, Scully asked, "Has it been determined what he died of?"

"She," Meecham told Scully brusquely. "Ganesha was a twelve-year-old Indian female. Far as I can see, she ran herself into the ground. Died of total exhaustion."

"How did she escape?" Scully asked.

Meecham wrinkled his brows. "Well, I gotta say it's a mystery. When I got the call that she was on the highway, I thought I'd find her cage open or something. But it was locked tight. Just like I left it the day before at closing time."

"Any idea how an elephant could have escaped a locked zoo cage?" Mulder asked.

"No sir," Meecham said. "No sign of tampering either."

Mulder and Scully traded looks.

Meanwhile, Meecham scratched his head at the damage in the street.

"What a mess," he said. "You'd think they'd clean it up."

"We asked the police to let us see it before any cleanup," Mulder explained.

"Well, I guess you know your job," Meecham said. "Me, animals are mine. Been at the zoo for thirty years."

"You know elephants, then?" said Mulder.

"I know all the critters in the zoo," said Meecham. "Like I said, that's my job."

"Then maybe you can give me some information," said Mulder.

"If it has to do with the zoo," Meecham said.

"I've read about something called the elephant rebellion," said Mulder. "There have been reports from zoos across the country. A growing number of cases of elephants behaving violently. Turning on their keepers. Wrecking their pens. Was Ganesha ever a problem?"

Meecham's face stiffened. "Elephants are very big, very willful animals," he said.

Mulder waited for him to go on, but Meecham stayed silent.

"So there *were* problems?" Mulder probed.

Meecham's mouth tightened. "I'm not the one to

18

ask," he said edgily. "The person you want to talk to about that is Willa Ambrose."

"Ambrose?" said Scully, making a note in her book. "Who is she? Someone at the zoo?"

"Yeah," Meecham said. He looked as if he had a bad taste in his mouth. "She's what you call a naturalist. The Zoo Board of Supervisors hired her last year."

"And her job?" asked Scully.

"She's supposed to make the zoo up-to-date," said Meecham. "You know, all the new stuff they're coming up with nowadays. She's supposed to be in charge now. Not that she ever worked in a zoo before. Not that she knows much about animals outside of books and maybe videos."

"But you do," said Mulder.

"I sure do," Meecham agreed.

"Elephants included?" Mulder said.

"Elephants included," Meecham affirmed.

"Then let me ask you this," Mulder said. "The damage here on the street. Is it something you think could have been done by an escaped elephant?"

"My honest opinion?" said Meecham. "Yes."

"You are sure of that?" Mulder said.

"Yes," Meecham repeated.

"Thank you," Mulder said, giving Scully a triumphant glance.

Meecham looked at his watch. "If you don't want me for anything else, I got to be heading back to the job," he said. "Feeding time."

"Thanks a lot for your cooperation," Mulder said. "We may have more questions later. You know, questions that Ms. Ambrose may not be able to help us with."

"Feel free," Meecham said. "Any time."

Mulder waited until Meecham had gotten into his truck and driven off. Then he got down on his hands and knees and started rummaging through the papers littering the ground near the shattered newsstand.

"What are you looking for, Mulder?" asked Scully, bracing herself for the answer.

"A local paper," said Mulder, not looking up. "I want to see if David Copperfield's appearing in town."

Chapter FOUR

"Not much of a crowd here today," Scully remarked, looking around her. She and Mulder had decided it was time to pay the zoo a visit.

"It's a weekday," Mulder said. "There's probably a better turnout on weekends."

"There should be," Scully said. "It looks like a nice place. Better than a lot of zoos I've seen. Some of them, ugh. You really feel sorry for the animals."

"Yeah," said Mulder. "You want to put the keepers in the cages."

The Fairfield Zoo did look like a pleasant place. The animals' cages were big and clean. The outside enclosures had trees, rock formations, and streams of running water that imitated natural surroundings. The animals seemed healthy and well fed. As Mulder and Scully went along winding pathways and in and out of buildings, hunting an attendant, they saw lions and panthers, pythons and jackals, rhino and llamas, flamingos and seals.

Scully paused by an outdoor enclosure. She looked through the bars at a huge Bengal tiger. It was pacing back and forth, its muscles rippling. When it saw Scully, it opened its jaws and roared.

Then, growling, it resumed its pacing.

"It's beautiful," Scully said. "It reminds me of that poem by William Blake.

Tiger! Tiger! burning bright
In the forests of the night.

"It is beautiful," agreed Mulder. He looked at the tiger's cage. "And a little sad."

"Maybe that's why I always feel funny at a zoo," said Scully. "Like something's wrong. The balance seems off. Take the way that tiger moves, back and forth, back and forth. And the way it seems to be looking off into the distance when it stops. It's like that with all the animals. They're made to have space around them, and it isn't here."

"A lot of people feel that way," said Mulder. "There's quite a protest movement against the whole idea of zoos."

The tiger turned toward them and roared again. Its wicked-looking teeth gleamed.

"Still, there's something to be said for iron bars," said Scully, stepping back from the fence.

At that moment Mulder spotted an attendant, an elderly man in a green uniform.

"Hi," said Mulder. "We've been looking for someone to tell us where to find Willa Ambrose. Not too many attendants working today."

The man shook his head. "Not too many working any day. Been a lot of cutbacks here. Money troubles. Don't know how long my job is safe, and I been here thirty years."

Then he remembered what the visitors wanted to know. "Willa Ambrose. I saw her a while ago near the bird houses, down past the polar bears. You might try looking there."

"Thanks," Mulder said.

"Seems the human animals here have their own troubles," he remarked as he and Scully headed off.

"Right," said Scully. "They're feeling squeezed too."

They passed an enclosure where polar bears splashed in a shallow pool to escape the heat of the sun, and came to a building marked AVIARY.

The bird house was spacious and high-ceilinged, filled with tropical plants and rock ponds. Bright-plumaged birds of every color filled the air with their cries.

There was only one person inside—a woman in her thirties, tall and slender, dressed in a crisp white shirt and faded jeans. She carried an armload of books and notebooks. But they seemed forgotten as she stood gazing fondly at the feathered creatures.

"Ms. Ambrose?" Scully asked.

"Yes, I'm Willa Ambrose," she answered, smiling politely.

"I'm Agent Dana Scully," Scully said. "This is Agent Mulder. We're with the F.B.I."

Willa's smile vanished. So did the warmth in her voice. "Yes?" she said.

"May we ask you a few questions?" Scully said.

"Is this about Ganesha?" Willa wanted to know.

"Yes," Mulder said. "We spoke to a Mr. Meecham. He works here, I believe."

"My chief of operations," Willa said.

"In any case, he seemed reluctant to answer some of our questions," Mulder said. "He told us to see you."

"He did?" Willa raised her eyebrows slightly. But she seemed pleased by the news. Her face and her voice thawed. "I'm sorry if I was abrupt. You took me by surprise. How can I be of help?"

"An employee of the Federal Highway Department was fatally injured recently," Scully said. "It seems possible that an escaped elephant from your zoo was involved in his death."

Willa's smile vanished again. "It was my understanding that eyewitnesses could not say how the man was killed," she said coldly.

Scully glanced at Mulder. Her look told him that he could carry the ball from here on in. The killer elephant idea was his idea, not hers. She couldn't blame Willa Ambrose for rejecting a notion that seemed not only off the track but off the wall.

Mulder picked up the questioning without missing a beat. "Actually, what we're trying to find out is how Ganesha escaped."

"What did Ed Meecham say?" Willa asked.

"He said the cage was locked, the same way he left it," Mulder said.

Willa shrugged. "What more can I tell you?"

A man was trampled to death," Mulder said. "Trampled to death by a very large animal. An elephant from your zoo was found forty-three miles from here. No one's blaming anybody. We're just trying to find out the facts leading up to the incident."

"Okay," said Willa. "I guess you guys are just doing your job. Why don't I show you Ganesha's pen? It'll tell you more than anything I can say."

The elephant pen was a short walk away. It was surrounded by a high fence of iron bars on three sides, and at the rear by a concrete wall. The gate in the fence was secured by a heavy lock.

"This is where Ganesha stayed when she wasn't in her habitat," Willa said.

"And where is her habitat?" asked Mulder.

"Through those big steel doors in the back of the pen," Willa said. "She'd be there during the day for the public to see. Then at night she'd be taken back to this side. The habitat is quite nice, actually. Care to take a look at it?"

"No, thanks," Mulder said. "The holding pen is what interests me at the moment. This is where she escaped from, right?"

"Seems so," Willa said.

"Who has the key to the lock?" asked Mulder.

"Only me and Ed Meecham," said Willa.

Then she noticed that Scully was looking up at the high iron fence.

"Elephants aren't very good jumpers, if that's what you're thinking," Willa told her.

"Actually, I was wondering why you had such a small pen for such a large animal," Scully said.

Willa did not look happy as she answered the question. "This zoo was built in the 1940s. Many pens and habitats are much too confining. I was hired to help redesign the facility. I plan to expand the animals' living spaces, make them more humane. But these things take time."

Mulder pointed to two heavy chains coming out of the ground. "What are they for?" he asked.

Willa looked even more uncomfortable. "Those are tie-downs," she said. "They're used to restrict an animal's movements."

"They were used on Ganesha?" asked Scully.

"No," said Willa firmly. "I stopped their use when I came to work here."

"Stopped their use by whom?" asked Mulder.

Willa's face hardened. "By Ed Meecham," she said, an edge in her voice. "He belongs to a different generation of zookeepers. Many of his practices are . . . not enlightened."

"How is your relationship with Mr. Meecham?" asked Mulder.

Willa gave a tight smile. "I'm his boss and I'm a woman," she said. "Ed doesn't like that combination much. He also doesn't like the way I run the zoo. But that's his problem."

"Would he be angry enough to commit an act of sabotage?" asked Scully. "Would he be angry enough to let an elephant out of its cage?"

There was a silence as Willa pondered the question.

From a distance came the sound of the tiger roaring again.

Chapter FIVE

Finally Willa shook her head. "I can't see Ed Meecham doing something like that," she said. "Not that he likes me much. Or that he likes the idea of the kind of zoo I want. But he does like his job. And this zoo is in trouble—money trouble. The city is cutting back funding, and we need private contributions to keep going. Any kind of scandal, and the contributions would stop. This place would go down the drain."

"Have you and Meecham talked about the elephant's escape?" asked Mulder. "How it could have happened? What the elephant might have done outside before she died?"

"No," Willa said. "Ed and I aren't exactly buddies. We're barely on speaking terms. Besides, Ed's pretty busy now. He has his hands full just dealing with the W.A.O."

"The W.A.O.?" said Scully.

"The Wild Again Organization," Mulder said.

Scully smiled to herself. She could count on Mulder for information like that. There wasn't a far-out group in the country, in the world, maybe in the universe, that Mulder didn't know about.

"Who are they?" she asked him.

"They're a group that believes any captive animal is a crime against nature," Mulder told her. "They also believe that they can break any human laws to stop this crime."

"They're going to have a field day with Ganesha," said Willa grimly. "In fact, they've already started. One of their leaders has set up shop out where that highway worker died. He's handing out leaflets to every driver who slows down to rubberneck."

"Who is he?" asked Mulder.

"A guy named Kyle Lang," said Willa.

Scully heard an odd note in Willa's voice when she said the name—a kind of wavering.

"You know him?" Scully asked.

Willa's mouth tightened. "We . . . She paused, then went on, "We've had a few run-ins."

"What sort of a person is he?" Scully asked.

"He's very committed," Willa said. "He sees things in terms of black and white. No shades of gray. You're either on his side or you're his enemy. He . . ." She paused again. "But you'll find out for yourself when you interview him—as I'm sure you will."

In the distance the tiger roared again.

"I'd better see if there's any trouble," Willa said. "Sometimes people get their kicks teasing the big cats. I'm trying to educate visitors not to be cruel, but it's tough." She sighed, then shrugged. "Gotta keep trying. You have to do the best you can. This world may not be perfect, but it's the only one we've got."

Mulder and Scully watched her walk off in the direction of the tiger enclosure.

"She seems dedicated to her job," Scully remarked. "She's facing tough odds, though. Budget cuts. An outdated facility. Angry old-timers. And this fellow Kyle Lang. I got the feeling he bothered her more than all the rest. Wonder why."

"Let's take Ms. Ambrose's advice," Mulder said. "Go meet Mr. Lang. If nothing else, his flyers should be interesting."

"Let's contact Washington first. See if there's a file on him," Scully said. "I have an idea there's something about him Willa wasn't telling us."

"Sure," said Mulder. "Though facts in the files and facts in the flesh can be very different things."

Kyle Lang stood with leaflets in his hand near the unfinished highway lane where Ray Hines had died.

Tall and lean, flannel-shirted and blue-jeaned, Kyle walked with the stride of a man at ease in his body and at home on the earth. He smiled at Scully and Mulder as they got out of their car, and extended a leaflet.

"Thanks. We'll read it later," Mulder said, putting it in his jacket pocket. "Right now we'd like to talk to you. And perhaps your friend over there."

Mulder indicated a young redheaded man leaning against the door of a beat-up truck parked up the highway. He looked barely out of his teens. He also looked permanently angry. There was a scowl on his face and a hostile look in his eyes.

"And you are?" asked Kyle.

"F.B.I. Agent Fox Mulder and my partner, Agent Dana Scully," Mulder said.

Mulder half expected Kyle to react to the information. Most people froze at least a second when they heard "F.B.I." But Kyle was unfazed. If anything, he looked slightly amused.

"Come to investigate the crime scene?" he asked. "You're in the wrong place. I suggest you try the zoo."

"We've already been there," said Mulder.

"Then you've seen the cage where Ganesha was kept," said Kyle. "Fifty feet by fifty feet. For an elephant."

"You consider that inhumane?" Scully asked.

"I consider it criminal," Kyle answered, all trace of amusement gone. "It would be like forcing you or me to live in a pickle barrel."

"Speaking of criminal actions," Scully said, "according to F.B.I. files, you've been arrested over a dozen times. For activities involving the kidnapping of zoo and circus animals."

"The W.A.O. sees it as liberation," Kyle said calmly.

"Were you involved in the liberation of Ganesha?" Scully asked.

"That would make me an accessory to murder, wouldn't it?" Kyle said.

There was a moment of silence.

Then Kyle said, "Sorry, G-people. I'm not confessing anything. Endangering an animal in any way is against everything the W.A.O. believes in. And elephants are especially precious forms of life."

"Really?" said Mulder, in a deliberately harsh tone. "I wouldn't have thought it. They've got such thick hides."

Scully knew what Mulder was doing. He was needling Kyle, trying to get under his skin. It was an excellent way to get a suspect to talk.

Scully joined in. "I always thought they were just big dumb brutes with a yen for peanuts," she said.

But Kyle didn't seem to get angry. He seemed interested only in setting them straight. "You couldn't be more wrong," he told them. "Elephants are incredibly gentle, spiritual, intelligent creatures. Their behavior and their rituals are a link to a past that no humans have ever witnessed. Do you know that they actually bury their dead? That they have graveyards hundreds and hundreds of years old? That they instinctively know where the bones of their ancient ancestors lie? And that we humans have no idea how?"

"You know a lot about elephants," said Mulder, smiling.

"I wish I knew more about them," Kyle said. About them and all animals. The more you know, the more you treasure them."

"But you must have some idea of the facts about Ganesha's escape," Mulder asked. "Where was she going? What was she running from?"

"You really want to know?" said Kyle.

"That's what we've come all this way for," Mulder said.

"Then come along with me," said Kyle. "I'll do better than tell you. I'll show you."

Chapter SIX

"Follow our truck," said Kyle. "It's a half hour's drive."

"Where are you taking us?" asked Scully.

"To a video show," Kyle told them. "Educational TV."

He went to his truck and spoke briefly to the red-headed young man. The two climbed into the truck's cab and drove off toward Fairfield.

Scully and Mulder followed, Scully driving. Halfway to town, she switched on the headlights. The sun was setting.

It was dark when they reached town and the run-down neighborhood where the truck parked. Scully parked behind it and she and Mulder got out.

Kyle and his friend were waiting for them in front of a ramshackle two-story building. On the front of the building hung a W.A.O. shingle. Kyle unlocked the front door and they all went inside.

"Welcome to our office," said Kyle. "As you can see, our organization isn't exactly well funded."

The second-floor office was filled with beat-up furniture, several aging computers, an old printer, a very old copying machine, and stacks of books, papers, posters, and leaflets. In the corner was a battered TV, topped with an equally battered VCR.

"Sit down and enjoy the show," Kyle said, pushing a video into the VCR. "I'll supply the commentary. Maybe Red here will add a few remarks. Probably not, though. Red believes in action, not words."

As Mulder and Scully sat down, Kyle started the video.

An elephant appeared on the screen. One of its tusks was chained close to the ground, forcing it to its knees. Its great head and trunk lay twisted sideways against the ground. Two trainers were prodding it from behind with long poles.

"The tie-down chain is called a martingale," said Kyle. "It's one of Ed Meecham's favorite devices. This is how he treats these majestic animals. Some animal lover. All he loves is his power over them."

Kyle froze the frame. Then he said, "You wanted to know what Ganesha was running from? Take a good long look. You wanted to know what she was looking for? Look in the dictionary. The word you want is *freedom*."

"This treatment is still going on?" Mulder asked.

"Meecham is a barbarian," Kyle said. "He's been torturing animals at the Fairfield Zoo for years. We're sure he's still at it."

"So you have proof?" Scully asked, turning to look at him.

Instead she met Red's eyes. They were filled with ice-cold hate. She shivered. She didn't have to hear Red say a word to know that he would do anything for his cause. His were the eyes of a true believer. A fanatic.

"We'll get our proof, don't worry," Kyle said.

"Maybe not," Mulder told him. "We've spoken to Willa Ambrose. She says she's put a stop to a lot of Meecham's old practices."

"Willa Ambrose?" Kyle sneered. "She's too busy with other things to keep tabs on Meecham."

"With what other things?" Scully asked.

"With a lawsuit she's fighting," Kyle said.

"Against whom?" asked Mulder.

"Against the government of Malawi in Africa," said Kyle.

"What are they fighting over?" asked Scully.

"Sophie," said Kyle.

"Sophie?" asked Scully.

"Sophie is a lowland gorilla," Kyle explained. "Willa rescued her from a North African customs house ten years ago. Smugglers were shipping her to a zoo in Europe. She was nearly dead from bad handling. Willa nursed her back to health and raised her like a child. But now the people in Malawi have tracked her down and want her back.

They claim they're starting a nature preserve and want to give Sophie a home. What they really mean is they want a tourist attraction. Tough luck for Willa. She loves that animal." But there was no sympathy in Kyle's voice. Quite the opposite.

"Then you think Malawi will win the case?" Mulder asked.

Kyle shrugged. "What does it matter? Either way, it's a perfect example of what humans do to animals. We turn them into objects for our own selfish pleasure."

"I thought you said Willa rescued this gorilla," said Scully.

Kyle snorted. "Rescued her so that Sophie could spend a life behind bars. Willa's duty was to return the gorilla to the wild. Because all animals should run free."

Scully was getting a little tired of Kyle Lang. Supporting a good cause was one thing. But being holier than thou was another. She said with an edge in her voice, "They should run free even if it means trampling a man to death?"

She made sure not to look at Mulder when she suggested Ganesha was the killer. She did not want to see the flicker of amusement in his eyes. She knew it too well. Sometimes she wished she didn't wind up agreeing with his theories so often.

"Maybe the guy should have gotten out of the

way," said Kyle, still with his irritating assurance.

"I'm sure he would have if he'd seen it coming," said Mulder quietly, almost to himself. Then he got to his feet. "Thank you for your time, Mr. Lang. "We'll be getting back to you."

Outside the building, Mulder said to his partner, "We're getting warm. Whatever's going on, it's all happening at the zoo, Scully."

"And now we know who's behind it," Scully said.

"Mr. Lang and his W.A.O.?" said Mulder. "You think they busted the elephant out?"

Scully heard the amusement in Mulder's voice. She answered with a flush of annoyance, "You heard what Kyle Lang said. All animals should run free. I'm talking facts that you can't deny."

"Then how do you explain some other facts?" Mulder inquired. "The eyewitness accounts? And the videotapes from the bank security camera? How do you explain why nobody actually saw the elephant until it was miles from the zoo?"

Scully did a fast mental run-through of the police report she had read. Then she said, "The lights at the road construction site were mercury vapor, ten thousand candlepower. In other words, half blinding. Certainly strong enough to limit a man's ability to adjust his vision to the dark. And the bank security cameras were poor quality. A gray elephant may not have registered as an image on the tape. Especially in the dim light in front of the building."

Mulder looked unconvinced.

"I don't know, Scully," he said. "Those guys may talk a good game. But that's what I think their game is. A lot of talk."

"Those guys are dedicated to just this kind of trouble making," Scully insisted. "You can't tell me that Kyle Lang isn't into the movement heart and soul. And did you take a good look at that kid Red? He looked like he'd run over his own mother to save a chipmunk. Not to mention the fact that they have some pretty high-tech gear, despite the crying about poverty. Did you spot that night-vision camera lying on a shelf?"

"Speaking of spying at night," said Mulder, glancing upward.

Scully followed his gaze. Looking down at them from the lighted second-floor window were Kyle and Red. Their mouths were hard and their eyes were narrowed. Their belief in gentleness and kindness clearly did not extend to the F.B.I.

Scully and Mulder walked down the street and around a corner.

As soon as they were safely out of sight, Scully stopped and said, "I wouldn't be surprised if they tried to keep the ball rolling."

"By doing what?" Mulder asked.

"Liberating another animal," Scully said. "Willa Ambrose said the zoo was having money troubles. The loss of another big exhibit might close it down for good. The W.A.O. would dance in the streets."

Mulder thought a moment, then nodded. "You might be right," he said. "Why don't you keep an eye on the W.A.O.? If there's any action, give me a ring on the cellular phone. I'll get mine out of the car."

"But where are you going?" Scully asked.

"To talk to the animals," Mulder told her.

Chapter SEVEN

Their names were Frohike, Byers, and Langley. But they went by a different name. They called themselves the Lone Gunmen. They aimed to shoot down official lies and blow the lids off coverups. They refused to believe even their own government. They kept hunting for dark forces beneath white-washes.

The media called them conspiracy freaks—paranoid oddballs who imagined evil everywhere.

Fox Mulder called them whenever he wanted information he couldn't get anywhere else.

Today he called them from a state-of-the-art telecommunication conference room in Fairfield. It was part of a big, gleaming new photocopying-and-faxing service center there. Even in Idaho, everything was getting up-to-date.

Outside the glass walls of the room, Mulder could see students and others feeding paper into copying machines. They showed no interest in him as he sat before a large video screen and punched out the number the Lone Gunmen had given him.

"Bingo," Mulder said to himself as the images of two men blinked to life on the screen.

There was Frohike, with his buzz-cut hair, his surplus olive-drab fatigues, and his Marine Corps–issue watch. With him was Byers, looking as if he should be selling insurance, a clean-cut straight arrow with a white shirt and striped tie.

"Beam me up, Scotty," Frohike wisecracked.

It was a typical beginning of a typical conversation with the Gunmen—weird, wired, and off the wall.

Mulder got into it without missing a beat. "Did anyone ever tell you the camera loves you, Frohike?"

"Yeah," Frohike said. "The arresting officers at the last protest rally I was at."

"So what's this costing the taxpayers, Mulder?" Byers cut in.

"A hundred and fifty dollars an hour," Mulder told him.

"Ouch," said Frohike. "Almost as much as one of the president's haircuts. Not nearly as much as a NASA toilet seat, though. Still, I'll remember next time I do my tax return."

"And when was the last time?" Mulder couldn't resist asking.

"Sorry, classified information," Frohike said. "Working for the Feds, I'm sure you know the term."

"By the way, where's Langley?" Mulder asked. Langley was the third Gunman.

"Sitting here off camera," Byers said. "Seems he has an objection to having his image bounced off a satellite. Who knows who might be watching? Nothing personal, you understand."

"Getting back to you, Mulder—what are you doing in Idaho?" asked Frohike.

"I'm on the job," said Mulder. "What do you guys know about the town of Fairfield?"

"Fairfield, Fairfield," mused Byers. "Let's see. No nerve gas plants. No missile silos. No underground nuclear waste dumps. But they do have a nice little zoo there. Lots of strange stuff going down. Animals escaping. Disappearing without a trace."

"Any idea how or why?" Mulder asked.

"You're not far from the Mountain Home Air Base," Frohike suggested, his eyes lighting up.

"Which means?" said Mulder.

"It's a major UFO hot spot," Frohike said.

"Here's a weird fact, Mulder," Byers put in. "No animal at Fairfield Zoo has ever had any offspring."

"Not a cub or a chick," said Frohike.

"A real mystery," Byers said. "I know of someone who might give you answers."

"Who?" asked Mulder.

"The woman who runs the zoo has a gorilla named Sophie," said Byers. "Sophie knows sign language. She has a vocabulary of over a thousand words. One thing about gorillas: Unlike humans, they always tell the truth."

At that moment Mulder's cellular phone rang.

"Wait a sec, guys. Got a call," he said to the two on the screen.

"If that's the lovely Agent Scully," Frohike said, "tell her I've been working out. I'm buff."

"Right," Mulder said. "I'm sure she'll be happy to hear it. Now if you can just convince her you're not crazy."

"That's your job, Mulder," Frohike said.

"I'll put it on my list of things to do—but right now duty calls," said Mulder. "If you'll excuse me." And he picked up the phone.

"Mulder, it's me," Scully whispered into the phone. She was standing in the shadows on the street next to the zoo.

"What's up?" Mulder asked.

"I was right," Scully told him. "I've followed the kid from the W.A.O. to the zoo."

"Red?" said Mulder.

"Nobody else but," Scully said. "He's going over the fence right now."

"I'm on my way, Scully," Mulder said. "Don't move."

"No way," Scully said. "I'm going after him. I want to find out what he's doing."

"But . . ." Mulder began. Then he realized it was useless to argue with Scully when it came to her doing her job. "Be careful" was all he could say.

"See you," said Scully, and hung up.

Moving fast, she headed for the fence that Red had gone over. Swiftly she scaled it. Working out in a gym might be a pain. But it paid off at times like this.

Inside the zoo grounds, she caught sight of the kid again. Wearing a backpack, he was going up the rock wall of an animal enclosure. Scully had to give him credit. He knew how to rock climb.

So did she. She let him get over, then went to the base of the rock wall. She tensed her muscles for the climb.

Then she froze as a hand brutally grabbed her shoulder from behind. It swung her around.

"What the devil do you think you're doing?" Ed Meecham demanded. He kept hold of her with one hand. In his other hand was a wicked-looking cattle prod. From the angry flush on his beefy face, she knew he'd be happy to use it on her.

"You've got a member of the W.A.O. on the premises," she told him.

Meecham's eyes narrowed. He tightened his grip on the cattle prod. He looked like a beast of prey scenting a kill.

"Come on," he said to Scully. "Let's get Willa

Ambrose. I want her to see me nab this guy. Maybe then she'll learn that they haven't repealed the law of the jungle yet. Sometimes you have to play rough."

"Is she near here?" Scully asked.

"Just a few steps away," said Meecham. "She's in her playhouse, with her best friend, as usual."

Meecham led Scully down a path to a window-less concrete building. On the door, a large sign said in big letters, SICK ANIMAL. AUTHORIZED PERSONNEL ONLY.

" 'Sick animal,' " Meecham sneered. "The only thing that's sick is *her*."

He opened the door without knocking and they went in.

The room inside was dimly lit by a single bulb. At one end was a large barred cage with its door open. Near the cage was a camp bed. Willa Ambrose was sitting on the bed. Beside her was a large gorilla.

Ambrose was exchanging gestures in sign language with the animal. Both of them stopped when they saw Meecham and Scully.

"It's okay, Sophie," Willa said soothingly to the animal. She turned to the intruders. "Meecham, I've told you never to come in here unless there's an emergency."

"Yeah," Meecham said with a note of triumph. "Well, there is an—"

46

That was as far as he got.

A tiger's roar filled the night.

And as Sophie leaped off the bed and ran for her cage, the whole zoo woke up.

Panthers and lions joined the roaring. Birds squawked and screeched. Monkeys chattered, wolves howled, and hyenas cackled hideously. The zoo sounded like an animal madhouse.

"We have to find out what's happening," Willa said. Swiftly she went out the door. Scully had to hand it to her. Willa did not show a trace of fear.

Holding his cattle prod ready, Meecham followed.

Scully was at his heels.

She didn't know what they would run into. But she was sure of two things.

It had something to do with Red.

And it wouldn't be good.

Chapter EIGHT

Red had loved animals as long as he could remember. As a child he had taken in stray cats and dogs and had fought with his mom to keep them. He had nursed injured birds back to health and joyfully watched them fly away. And he had been sick to his stomach when his dad had taken him on a deer hunt for the first and last time.

Anyone who hurt an animal filled him with rage. An animal in a cage was torture to him.

He and the W.A.O. were made for each other. Maybe he hadn't been able to make his mom take in strays. Maybe he hadn't been able to stop his dad from gunning down deer. But he would help show the world that animals should be safe and free.

He was looking forward to his job tonight. Dropping down on the far side of the rock wall, he reached into his backpack. He pulled out a night-vision video camera. It was a lovely piece of equipment. It was worth more than the W.A.O. could afford, but Red had a real talent for heisting. Not that he liked being a thief. But animal rights ranked way ahead of human laws in Red's book.

Inside the enclosure, he moved swiftly toward a

cage near the far wall. He looked into it. The yellow eyes of the Bengal tiger stared, unblinking, back at him. The big animal stood tensely, watching the stranger's every move.

"Hi, tiger—snarl for the camera," Red said softly. He pointed the camera and pressed the Start button. His video shoot tonight would capture the cruel sight of the magnificent cat in captivity. It would open the eyes of the world to the horror.

But suddenly the tiger and the cage started to swim before his eyes.

Waves of heat like those that rise from desert sands made his eyes water. The tiger and the cage were melting away.

Red blinked. He rubbed his eyes. He tried to focus them—and was blinded by white light exploding.

The light faded, and his vision returned.

His mouth dropped open.

The cage was empty.

"Where is the—?" he started to ask himself.

A huge roar came from behind him.

A tiger's roar.

Red whirled around and saw—nothing.

It's gotten out somehow, he thought. *It's in the dark somewhere. It doesn't know I'm a friend. I gotta get out of here before—*

That was the last thing he thought before a smashing force knocked him off his feet.

It was like being hit by a car.

But he still could see nothing. Nothing except the red light of the video camera on the ground. The camera had flown from his hands, but it was still taping.

Stunned, he managed to sit up. Pain seared his chest. He looked down. His shirt had been slashed open. He put his hand into the opening. It came out covered with blood.

Then came another roar, even louder than the first.

Red staggered shakily to his feet. He started to stumble away.

Again he was batted down.

This time he didn't get up. Not on his own, at least.

He was picked up like a limp rag doll and tossed through the air.

His body landed and was picked up and tossed again.

And again.

And again.

Until playtime was over.

And Red lay still for good.

That was the way he was lying when Willa, Meecham, and Scully found him. The blood on his chest and face glistened in Meecham's flashlight beam.

"My God," Willa said. "Poor kid."

"Guess he found out a tiger isn't a tabby cat," muttered Meecham.

Scully shook her head. She had seen a lot of corpses in her career. This was one of the worst.

Out of the dark, Mulder's voice asked, "What's happened?"

He reached them and looked down at Red.

"Sorry I'm late. I got here as fast as I could," he said to Scully.

"Doubt you could have done anything," said Scully. "It all happened so fast. I thought I would give the kid enough rope to hang himself. But this wasn't what I had in mind."

"Nothing to do now but call the police," Willa said. "And try to fend off the reporters."

"Plus hunt down that cat on the loose," said Meecham.

"There's one other thing to do as well," said Scully. "And I'm sure the police will agree."

"What's that?" asked Mulder.

"Pay Mr. Kyle Lang a visit."

Scully had disliked Kyle Lang at first sight.

She liked him even less when she went to see him again.

She had told Mulder that she would take personal pleasure in grilling the W.A.O. leader. Mulder told her to have fun. He would check out other leads.

Kyle kept a poker face when Scully and two sheriff's deputies showed up at his office. He sat at his desk, leaning back in his chair, as Scully questioned him. He looked a little bored.

"Why was Red at the zoo?" Scully demanded.

"Don't know what you're talking about," Kyle said.

"You have no idea what he was doing," Scully pressed him.

"Not the faintest," Kyle said.

Scully showed him the video camera found at the scene of the slaying.

"What if I told you I saw this camera up there on your shelf yesterday?" she said.

"Guess I never noticed," Kyle answered blandly.

Scully fought to keep the rising anger out of her voice. "A tiger is missing. And a member of your organization is dead. For a man who claims to be so tenderhearted, you show a suprising lack of emotion."

Kyle shrugged. "If the tiger killed this person, it was a natural act."

Scully glared at him. "If I find evidence that Red was releasing animals under your orders," she said, "I'll make sure you go to prison and spend your life in a cage."

Kyle met her gaze without flinching. Scully had seen cool customers before. But this guy was an iceberg.

She was trying to think of some way to melt his icy resistance when Mulder came into the office.

He was holding an evidence bag. He tapped it and motioned for Scully to follow him.

"Okay, guys, it's your turn," she said to the deputies. "See if you can make him squirm."

She left the room with Mulder as one of the deputies took her place. "That guy really gets my goat," she told Mulder, her hands clenched into fists.

Mulder glanced at her fists. "You okay, Scully?"

Scully took a deep breath and exhaled slowly. She let her hands go limp. "Yeah," she said.

"All calmed down?" Mulder asked.

"Yeah, yeah, I get your message," said Scully impatiently. "I'll be a good levelheaded agent. Now fill me in. They find the tiger?"

"No," Mulder said. "But I viewed the cassette from Red's camera. It was going when he got killed. And it shows he wasn't killed by a tiger."

"What?" Scully exclaimed.

"Unless it's trick photography, the kid was killed by some kind of invisible phantom," Mulder said calmly.

"But you saw the body, Mulder," Scully protested.

"That kid was mauled to death. He had deep claw marks on his chest and back. It had to be the tiger."

"I can't explain it, Scully," Mulder said. "But I think I know someone who can."

"Who?" asked Scully.

"Can't you guess?" asked Mulder.

"No," said Scully. "Tell me."

Mulder smiled. "I don't want to spoil the surprise."

Chapter NINE

"I think we'll find her here," Mulder said.

He and Scully stood before the zoo door marked SICK ANIMAL. AUTHORIZED PERSONNEL ONLY.

"So you figure Willa Ambrose has been keeping stuff to herself," said Scully.

Mulder's only answer was a smile. He raised his hand to knock on the door.

Before he could knock, Scully said, "Mind giving me your reasons, Mulder? Call me insecure, but when I go to see a suspect, I like to know why."

"You'll find out soon enough," Mulder assured her. Again he raised his hand to knock.

Before he could knock, the door swung open. Willa Ambrose faced them. She was just going out. When she saw them, her mouth tightened and her body stiffened.

"Ms. Ambrose, may we have a word with you?" said Mulder.

"I don't know anything more than I've already told the police," Willa said. "I have nothing else to say."

"I understand this is where you keep Sophie—your gorilla," Mulder said.

"Sophie is ill," Willa said curtly. She clearly wanted to cut the conversation short.

"Can we meet her?" Mulder asked.

Willa said nothing. But her hostile stare said a lot.

"We're not here to take her away from you," Mulder assured her.

Willa looked hard at Mulder. She bit her lip, hesitating.

"All right. Come in," she said, leading Mulder and Scully inside to the gorilla's cage.

Sophie was crouched in the rear of the cage. She stared suspiciously at the visitors. This was the first time Scully had had a chance to take a good long look at her. Scully wondered why so big and powerful a creature should seem so fearful. Especially since Sophie had to be used to human beings by now.

"Six weeks ago, I had to take her out of her public habitat," Willa said, as if she were reading Scully's mind. "She had become withdrawn and depressed. She would ball herself up in the back corner of her cage and just shiver."

"Have you asked her why?" Mulder said.

Scully shot Mulder a look. Mulder's questions often took bizarre turns. But this one was really around the bend.

Willa seemed to find nothing strange about it.

She answered matter-of-factly, "I ask her all the time."

"What does Sophie say?" Mulder asked.

Willa's hands made a few quick signs. Then she translated them. " 'Light afraid.' Which means she's afraid of the light."

"She *speaks* to you!" Scully said.

"Over six hundred words, using American Sign Language," Willa said. "She understands over a thousand."

Willa found a piece of paper on her desk and handed it to Scully. "You might find this interesting," she said. "It's a recent article on the subject."

Scully read it quickly. The article described studies conducted around the world of gorillas who had indeed mastered sign language.

She looked up from the article and saw Mulder smiling again. Now she understood why.

"Is this who you wanted talk to? A gorilla?" she demanded.

"I suggest you read your F.B.I. training manual again, Scully," he told her. "It's a basic rule. 'Question all possible witnesses.' "

"But a gorilla!" Scully exclaimed. "What could a gorilla know?"

"Perhaps Ms. Ambrose can answer that," Mulder said.

"Gorillas are extremely sensitive creatures," Willa said. "Sophie's language skills make her even more so."

"But why would she be afraid of the light?" Scully said.

Willa gave Scully a sharp look. "You've talked to Kyle Lang?" she asked.

"Yes. A couple of times," Scully said.

"Then there's no sense in beating around the bush," Willa said. "I'm sure he's told you about my trouble with the Malawi government. There's a chance Sophie could be taken away from me. I think she knows it. And she's scared. In her mind, Africa may conjure up a picture of light. It never ceases to amaze me how Sophie can put things together."

Scully looked at the gorilla again. Sophie was still crouched in the back of the cage. Scully saw for the first time how alert the animal's eyes were. How they seemed to take in everything that was happening. Scully still couldn't fully believe that animals could actually think. On the other hand, she no longer was absolutely sure that they couldn't.

"It is a possibility," Scully conceded.

She turned to see if Mulder agreed. But his attention had shifted elsewhere. He was examining crayon drawings taped to a wall. They looked as if they had been made by a preschooler.

"Are these drawings Sophie's?" he asked.

"Yes," Willa said. "She's always liked to draw. Though she hasn't done any new ones for a while. Not since she became ill."

"Interesting drawings," said Mulder. "They seem to repeat the same pattern over and over again. A small brown blob in a circle. Any idea what it might mean?"

"I can't be sure, but I have a strong hunch," Willa said. "Up until recently, Sophie desperately wanted a baby. The brown object in the circle was her way of showing it."

"Have you ever attempted to mate her?" Mulder asked.

"I was looking for a suitable partner," said Willa. "But then the Malawi government got into the act. With all the stress on Sophie, I didn't think it wise to go ahead. I decided to put the project on hold until everything was settled."

Mulder nodded. He was looking at her intently, following her words closely.

"Let me make sure I understand you," he said. "Sophie showed strong signs of wanting a baby. Then she seemed to stop wanting one. And at the same time, she started being spooked by some kind of light."

"That's right," Willa said. "Her desire to become pregnant was clearly diminished by some kind of stress."

"Uh-huh," Mulder said. "That's one explanation at least. One among several." He paused a moment, thinking. Then he said, "I was told there never has been a successful pregnancy at the Fairfield Zoo."

"I knew I could count on Kyle Lang to keep you fully informed," said Willa with a grimace.

"Is it true?" Mulder asked.

"Yes," she said. "But I don't think it's for the reasons that Kyle claims. Not because of anything Ed Meecham has done to these animals."

"Why, then?" Mulder persisted.

"For an animal to bear young is always difficult in captivity," she said.

"But a perfect failure rate?" pressed Mulder.

"I know," Willa said. "It looks bad. It's one of the things I was determined to change when I came here."

Mulder nodded and Scully saw a familiar gleam in his eyes. She started to pay even closer attention as he continued his questioning.

"Was there ever an attempt made to mate Ganesha?" he asked.

"No," Willa said. "Mating elephants out of the wild is rarely successful. There have been only six elephant births in captivity in the last ten years."

Scully saw Mulder's face light up. She braced herself. She did not know what Mulder's latest brainstorm was. But she knew from experience that she should be ready for anything.

Anything except the expected, at least.

"Do you have a veterinary facility here?" Mulder asked.

"Yes," she said. "We have an excellent animal hospital. Bringing it up to date was one of the first things I did."

"Ms. Ambrose," Mulder said, "I have a rather unusual request for you. But it might help to explain what's been going on here."

Then he turned to Scully.

"I'm going to need your help too," he said. "I can promise you it will be a most interesting challenge for your skills."

Scully thought she had never seen Mulder look quite so eager.

"I bet it will," she said.

Chapter TEN

"Mulder, this isn't exactly in my job description," Scully said.

She was wearing protective plastic gear, complete with hood. A surgical mask dangled around her neck. In her hand was a scalpel. It shined brightly in the glaring lights of the operating room.

"An oversight," said Mulder. "You have everything you need for the job. A degree in medicine. A degree in science. What more could you want?"

"A degree of sanity," said Scully. Mulder had told her in private what her assignment was, but she still couldn't believe it. "This is the craziest thing you've ever asked me to do."

Mulder started to answer. But his voice was drowned out by an ear-splitting whine. It came from an electric saw.

He and Scully looked down from the scaffolding on which they stood.

Below them was a gaping hole.

The hole opened into the huge body of an elephant.

A dead elephant.

Ganesha.

The whining came from inside that hole. After a minute it stopped. A figure in protective gear and mask, wearing a miner's helmet, emerged.

"How did it go?" Mulder asked.

"I've carved the ribs away," Willa Ambrose answered, laying aside her saw. "There's room for both of us now, Agent Scully."

Scully turned to Mulder. "I hope you know what you're doing." Then she added, "I should say, what *I'm* doing."

"I'm pretty sure of what we're going to find," Mulder said.

"Pretty sure isn't enough for this job," said Scully. She sighed. "But I guess it'll have to do."

Scalpel in hand, Scully climbed down to join Willa.

Working side by side, the two used their scalpels on the inside of the elephant. Slice by slice they carved their way toward the rear of the corpse.

"I'm glad you know your way around animals," Scully grunted to Willa as they tunneled away. "I'd hate to get lost down here."

"Well, I'm lost myself in a way," Willa said. "I mean, you told me what you're looking for. But I don't have a clue what you expect to find." She reached into the opening they had made. From it she pulled a large, dripping body organ.

She handed it to Scully, "Now maybe you'll let

me in on the secret," she said. "What exactly do you hope to learn from Ganesha's uterus?"

"Can't you guess?" Scully said.

"Considering the functions of the uterus, one possibility does come to mind," Willa said. "But I won't even mention it. It's too weird to take seriously."

An hour later, in the laboratory, Scully looked up from a high-power medical microscope.

"You were right, Mulder," she said.

Willa was watching. "What did you find?" she asked.

"You want to tell her, Mulder?" said Scully. "Or should I?"

"You're the doctor," Mulder said.

"Ganesha had been pregnant," Scully said.

"What do you mean," said Willa, "when you say she *had* been pregnant?"

"She was no longer pregnant at the time of her death," Scully said.

"Then you're saying that not only was she pregnant—but she also gave birth." Willa struggled visibly to make sense of it all.

"Exactly," Scully said.

"I don't believe you," Willa declared.

"See for yourself," Scully said, making room for her at the microscope. "See the traces of the offspring on the uterus wall? And the place where it exited?"

Willa looked into the microscope. "I don't care what it looks like," she said. "It's impossible."

"Of course it is," Mulder said. "But so is an invisible elephant. Unless you're prepared to look at things from a different angle."

"What is going on here?" Willa demanded, shaking her head in disbelief.

"Whatever it is, it's been going on for some time," Mulder said. "And I think you're going to see evidence of the same thing when we find your missing tiger."

"So you've come up with a theory about the case," Scully said.

"I want more proof before I make it official," Mulder said. "You know the brass. They still find cases like this hard to swallow."

Willa had been totally left behind. "Is this some kind of joke?" she asked.

"I'm afraid there's nothing funny about this case," said Mulder.

As if to emphasize his words, sirens sounded in the distance.

"A fire somewhere," Willa guessed.

"Those are police sirens," said Scully.

"I'm sure you know better than I," Willa said. "It's quite unusual to hear them around here. Except that recently everything has become so unusual."

"Which is why we'd better follow them," said Mulder, heading for the door.

Scully and Willa had to half run to keep up with his long-legged stride as he made tracks for the rental car outside.

"I'll drive," he told Scully.

As she got in beside him, she told Willa, "Better use your safety belt, even in the back. For somebody in law enforcement, my partner is not exactly into speed limits."

The seat belts had barely clicked shut when Mulder started the car with a screech. It tore out of the parking lot toward the sound of the sirens.

"Any idea what's in this direction?" Mulder asked Willa. "What the trouble spot might be?"

"The only place I can think of is the new shopping plaza," she said.

The wailing sirens were closer now—much closer.

They turned a corner.

"Watch out!" Scully warned Mulder.

Mulder was already stopping the car.

A crowd of people ran down the street toward them—men, women, and children with terror on their faces.

"Let's see what's up," said Mulder.

He was out of the car fast, with Scully and Willa close behind.

By this time most of the crowd had passed.

A woman carrying a small child in her arms

paused to warn them, "Not in that direction! The other way, fast!"

Before they could ask any questions, she was running again. At the far end of the street, where she'd come from, were two squad cars, sirens blaring, red lights flashing.

"It's the shopping plaza," Willa said, "just beyond the squad cars."

Mulder and Scully broke into a run, with Willa on their heels. At the squad cars they found six officers with drawn weapons.

Scully looked past them at the shopping plaza. She felt a chill run through her.

The plaza was gleaming new. It had a six-screen movie house, expensive stores whose windows were packed with goods, sit-down restaurants and fast-food places offering everything from Tex-Mex to Chinese. But now it was empty. The only traces of life were a few discarded paper plates and other litter on the rust-colored brick pavement. The only movement came from the bright dancing images on a row of TV sets playing in a store window. The scene was spooky, silent as a graveyard.

"Get back, mister," a cop commanded. "This area is off-limits."

"F.B.I.," Mulder said, and both he and Scully flashed their ID.

"What's the trouble, Officer?" Scully asked.

"Nothing for the F.B.I. to worry about," the cop said.

"Unless the Feds are into hunting tigers," added his partner.

Chapter ELEVEN

"The tiger's been sighted!" Willa exclaimed.

"You know about it?" said the first cop, surprised. "I gotta hand it to you. You Feds are on the ball."

"I'm not connected with them," Willa said, indicating Mulder and Scully. "I'm Willa Ambrose, director of the zoo. I'm the one who phoned the police to report that the tiger had escaped."

"Yeah," the cop said. "We went looking for you to get details. But we couldn't find you. Where were you?"

"I was taking care of an animal in our hospital. An emergency," Willa said, and swiftly changed the subject. "Who spotted the escaped animal?"

"Some guy chowing down on a Big Mac in the plaza," the cop said. "He said he saw the tiger appear out of nowhere, walking right through the shoppers. He gave our emergency number an instant call. We got here in minutes. But by that time the panic was on."

"Yeah," Scully said. "We were almost knocked over in the stampede."

"That must have been the last wave of people

running for their lives," the cop said. "It took a few minutes for word to get around."

"And the tiger—where is it now?" asked Mulder.

"I wish I knew," said the cop. "We've blocked off all streets leading out of the plaza. But it might already have gotten out. I understand those things move fast."

"When they have to," Willa said. "When they're hunting—or fleeing."

"We'll catch up with it," the second cop promised. "And when we do, we're ready to handle it." He patted his rifle.

"That won't be necessary," Willa said. She opened her large handbag. Scully had wondered why she needed it. Now she had her answer. Willa pulled out an impressive pistol.

"Thanks for your offer, Ms. Ambrose." The first cop smiled. "But we have all the firepower we need."

"You don't understand," Willa said. "We shouldn't kill the animal for simply obeying her instincts. It's not her fault that she's out of her natural environment. It's ours. There's no need to use bullets on her. This pistol shoots a tranquilizer dart. It will put her out of action without injuring her."

"You really think that'll stop it?" he said dubiously. "I saw that thing when I took my kids to the zoo. It's a monster."

"I know it'll work, Officer," Willa said firmly.
"I've used this gun before."

"Well, if you say so, ma'am." He sounded unconvinced.

"Funny thing," said his partner. "The guy at the
zoo didn't say anything about tranquilizer guns. In
fact, he asked if he could join the hunt with his
shotgun. Let's see, what was his name?"

"Meecham," Willa said shortly. "Ed Meecham.
He works at the zoo. But I outrank him. I'm in
charge there."

"Yes, ma'am," the first cop said.

"But we'll still keep our guns out, just in case,"
his partner said.

Willa opened her mouth to argue further—but
the squad car's radio blared.

"All-car alert! All-car alert!" a female voice said
loud and clear. "Tiger sighted at Dumont and Spencer!
Tiger sighted at Dumont and Spencer! Proceed there
immediately! Proceed there immediately!"

"Come on!" the first cop said to his partner.

"Right," his partner said. "That's twenty blocks
downtown. That tiger moves like the wind."

The two cops hurried to get into the squad car.

"Mind if we tag along?" Mulder asked.

"Sure, plenty of room," the first cop said.

Mulder, Scully, and Willa crammed themselves

into the backseat. Willa kept her pistol on her lap.

Siren wailing, the squad car joined the others racing across the city.

"Here we are," the cop in the driver's seat said. "Dumont and Spencer."

But no streets signs were needed. At least half a dozen squad cars were already there, their lights flashing.

"Not a good idea," Willa said as they got out. "The animal will be scared to death. It'll just make her harder to approach."

"There's another possibility," Scully said. "I don't know that tigers are any different from humans when they're threatened. It's flight or fight. You can never be sure which."

"One thing is sure," said Mulder, looking around him. "The animal has a great hiding place—or hunting ground."

The corner of Dumont and Spencer was the site of a high-rise construction project. A huge hole had been dug. Nearby a thicket of steel beams rose toward the sky, linked here and there by newly built floors and ceilings. Workers in hard hats milled around in confusion. The authorities in Fairfield, thought Scully, were not highly trained in handling major emergencies.

"Right," she said to Mulder. "It's a perfect place for a tiger to roam. A man-made jungle."

Willa said nothing. But she kept her tranquil
izer gun ready as she looked around the site.

Suddenly her face hardened.

She strode over to a group of sheriff's deputies.
They all carried shotguns. With them was Ed
Meecham. He had a shotgun too.

Willa faced Meecham head-on.

"Put that gun away, Ed," she said. "And you can
tell the local Wyatt Earps to do the same."

Meecham kept a firm hold on his shotgun. "You
want another death on your hands, Ms. Ambrose?"
he demanded.

"That cat can be captured without harm to anyone," she told him.

"This is no time for wishful thinking," Meecham
replied.

"As your superior, I'm ordering you, Ed," Willa
said, her voice like a hammer pounding in a nail.

Meecham stiffened, then shrugged. With a sneer
in his voice he answered, "Yes, ma'am. You're the
boss. Anything you say."

She gave him one last hard look. Then she
headed into the maze of construction.

A cop tried to stop her.

"The cat may be anywhere in there, ma'am," he
warned.

"Don't worry," Willa told him. "I have the equipment to handle her."

The cop started after her, but Mulder stopped him.

"Don't worry, Officer," he said, flashing his ID. "Agent Scully and I will provide her with backup."

Mulder pulled out his pistol. Scully did the same. They hurried after Willa.

"How many darts does your gun hold?" Scully asked when they caught up with her.

"One," she said.

"Will that be enough?" asked Scully.

"Yes," Willa said. "It has to be."

Scully dropped back to fall into step with Mulder.

"I'm all for saving the animals, Mulder," Scully said to him in a half whisper. "But just one dart? You know what I mean?"

Mulder nodded. Without a word both of them released the safety catches on their weapons.

Suddenly a burly worker came racing out of the unfinished building.

"It's there," he said, white-faced.

Willa peered into the site and raised her dart gun.

"I think I see her tail!" she exclaimed. She dashed into the unfinished building, dodging a huge girder.

Her sudden movement caught Mulder and

Scully by surprise. By the time they moved to follow her, she was out of sight.

Then they heard her voice. "Over here!"

They walked through a forest of girders in the direction of her voice. But they still couldn't see her.

Then they heard her again—much closer.

This time the sound of her voice was a scream.

They raced toward it.

Then they heard another sound.

A shattering shotgun blast.

They ran around a girder and finally saw Willa.

She stood white-faced and trembling, her gun at her side.

Beside her stood Ed Meecham, his shotgun smoking.

Less than five feet away lay the tiger. Blood streamed from a bullet hole between its eyes.

"She was hiding up there," Willa gasped, indicating an unfinished ceiling. "She leaped at me from behind."

She was shaking too hard to go on.

"Thought I'd keep an eye on you," Meecham said. "There are things I know about animals that you don't." He shook his head. "They don't all talk and draw pictures."

Chapter TWELVE

Mulder read the sign on the zoo entrance.

ZOO CLOSED TO THE PUBLIC UNTIL FURTHER NOTICE.

Mulder gave the sign a crooked smile as he passed it. Ed Meecham had saved Willa Ambrose's life. But Meecham hadn't been able to save Willa's job. Or his own.

Mulder walked through the zoo, hunting Willa. He wanted to tell her what Scully had found when she cut open the dead tiger.

Scully had asked Mulder to give Willa the news by himself. She had had enough of zoos for a while. She was going to clean things up at the animal hospital lab, then get some sleep. She just hoped she didn't see the tiger in her dreams. Such a beautiful animal, and so dead. She feared it might haunt her.

Mulder found Willa with a group of men and women in suits. They were standing near a whale tank, watching a pair of orcas swimming to and fro. Now and then the whales' mouths opened, revealing rows of evil-looking teeth.

The people with Willa didn't look much kinder. Their eyes glittered coldly as they shook hands with her and left.

Only then did she notice Mulder.

"Well, that's that," she said. "The tiger was the last straw. They've cut off all funding to the zoo. They've arranged to ship the animals to other zoos. My last job here will be to get them crated up."

"I'm sorry," Mulder said.

"Not as sorry as I am," said Willa. "The timing couldn't be worse."

Mulder saw the pain in her eyes. "You mean for Sophie," he said.

Willa nodded. "What I had in my favor was my job here," she said. "I was able to guarantee her a good home."

Her face started to melt. Then, with effort, she pulled herself together. "But that's my problem, not yours," she told Mulder. "You have your own problems. Tell me, did the results come back on the tiger?"

"Scully says the animal definitely had been pregnant."

Willa shook her head firmly. "Impossible. There's no chance these animals could have gotten pregnant. No way."

"What if they were made pregnant by injection? By artificial insemination?" Mulder suggested.

"It's a very complicated procedure," Willla said. "I would have known."

"Unless it was done somewhere else," Mulder said.

Willa looked lost.

Mulder made himself clearer. "What do you know about alien abduction?"

"You're kidding me, right?" Her eyes widened.

Mulder said nothing.

"You actually think these animals are being taken aboard spaceships?" she asked.

But Mulder couldn't be stopped by a look that said he was crazy. There came a point in a case when he had to state the facts as he saw them. They had reached that point.

"I don't know where the animals are being taken," he said. "But there seems to be trouble getting them back. Perhaps there's a technical foul-up, some hitch in a space-time-energy hookup. In any event, according to a computer analysis of available data, the animals are being returned roughly two miles west-southwest of the zoo."

"Aliens making animals pregnant?" said Willà, trying to get a handle on the idea.

"And stealing the results," replied Mulder.

"But why?"

"Who knows?" said Mulder. "Maybe they've been observing us. Maybe they see what we're doing to the planet. Poisoning the sea. Cutting down the forests. Plowing up the grasslands. Spraying insecticides on food sources. Slaughtering animals for food, furs, hides, ivory, or simple pleasure. Destroying whole species and locking up the ones still alive."

"So say—for the sake of argument—that they know what we're doing—and I won't argue about that," Willa said. "So what?"

"Maybe they're making a kind of Noah's Ark," Mulder said. "Maybe they want to save the animals left in the world from extinction."

"What an idea!" said Willa, blinking.

"I'm just guessing at their motive," Mulder said. "But I'm almost positive that they're the reason why there's never been a successful birth at this zoo. They've gotten here first."

It took less than a moment for Willa to make up her mind about Mulder's brilliant idea. "I think that's the most ridiculous thing I've ever heard," she declared.

Mulder didn't back off. "If you don't believe me, then ask Sophie."

"You think this is what she's so afraid of?" said Willa.

"I think Sophie is pregnant," Mulder said. "And she's afraid of them taking the baby."

"Ridiculous," said Willa again. But now her voice wavered.

"Then prove it," Mulder said. "If you dare."

That last word decided it. "Follow me, Agent Mulder," said Willa.

She unlocked the door marked SICK ANIMAL, and Mulder followed her inside.

Sophie was in the rear of her cage. She stared at the visitors suspiciously.

She relaxed only when she heard Willa's voice. "Sophie, come here. There's something I want to ask you."

Cautiously Sophie moved toward the human being she loved most in the world. But in the middle of the cage she stopped and looked past Willa at Mulder. She started to make quick, nervous signs.

"What's she saying?" Mulder asked.

" 'Man woman hurt,' " Willa said. "She thinks you and your partner are here to hurt her. Or me."

Willa made signs back to Sophie, saying as her hands moved, "Man woman are here to help you. They want to know about Sophie's baby."

Sophie stiffened, then retreated. She crouched in the back of the cage, making anguished grunts, her eyes big with fright, her long arms curled protectively around her stomach.

"Seems she got the message," said Mulder.

"And it seems you're right—about her being pregnant, anyway," said Willa.

"Can I ask her something?" Mulder asked. "Can she understand simple words?"

"Probably," Willa said. "Try it and see."

Mulder spoke slowly and clearly. "Sophie—do you want to leave here?"

Sophie became still.

She looked at Mulder and he looked straight back at her.

Then she signaled her reply.

"She says, 'light afraid,'" Willa translated. Then she asked Sophie, "What are you afraid of?"

Sophie made more signs and started to tremble again.

"'Baby go flying light,'" said Willa in a stunned voice. "That could mean . . . that is, if you're actually right about aliens trying to—"

Mulder started to say something, but Willa's raised hand stopped him. Then she rubbed her hand across her forehead.

"Let me try to put this all together," she said. "It seems so incredible. It's so hard to—"

Just then the door swung open.

It was Scully.

"Ms. Ambrose," she said. "I thought I'd find you here. I'm afraid I have bad news."

"God, what now?" Willa said.

"I've just come from the lab," Scully said, closing the door behind her. "There was a sheriff's deputy who came looking to serve you with papers. I think it's about Sophie."

"Oh, no," Willa said, going pale.

"He's waiting outside," Scully told her.

"What am I going to do?" Willa said.

"Whatever you do, Ms. Ambrose, you can't leave

Sophie here," Mulder said. "Not if you want her to be safe."

"But I've nowhere else to take her," Willa said.

There was a knocking at the door. Willa took a long look at Sophie huddled in the cage. Sophie looked back at her. There were no signs or words exchanged. Just love.

Then Willa slowly went to open the door.

The man waiting said, "Willa Ambrose?"

"Yes," she said.

The man thrust of a piece of paper into her hand. "I'm serving you with a court order," he said. "You are to release a gorilla named Sophie into protective custody."

He left her standing there with the paper in her hand and her face bleak with despair.

But as she turned to look at Sophie again, her jaw firmed.

Mulder recognized the look on her face.

It was the look of a gambler with one card left to play.

Mulder knew better than to ask what her ace in the hole was.

The stakes she was playing for were too high.

Mulder was able to decipher the sign she made to Sophie.

"I love you."

Chapter THIRTEEN

Kyle Lang heard an urgent knocking on the door. He got up from his desk and opened it.

"Willa," he said. "What brings you here this time of night? In fact, what brings you here at all?"

Willa stepped into the W.A.O. office quickly, closing the door behind her.

"I had to wait until no one would see me," she said. "But I had to talk to you."

"Willa, I'm touched, really touched. After all this time, you still care," Kyle said mockingly. Then he stopped joking. "What do you want? That I lay off the zoo? That I shouldn't kick it when it's down? Sorry, but I want to make sure it stays down—and out."

"Kyle, forget the zoo," Willa said. "I'm asking you to help me. You're my last hope."

"Hope for what?" asked Kyle.

"They're coming to take Sophie away from me," Willa said frantically.

"If you're looking for sympathy, look somewhere else." Kyle's voice was cold.

Then he saw the pain in her eyes. "Let her go, Willa," he said more softly.

"They're putting her in an iron cage as we speak," Willa said. "Without bars or windows.

They're taking her to the warehouse. It'll kill her."

"Sophie has spent her whole life behind bars," Kyle said. "Let her go home, Willa. She'll have the freedom she deserves."

"Freedom to do what?" Willa asked angrily. "To be killed by poachers? Who'll cut off her hands to sell to tourists?"

"Malawi promises to put her in a nature preserve," Kyle said.

"You know what that promise is worth," Willa said. "Malawi can't even police the streets of its capital, much less its forests."

"Freedom is worth a little danger," Kyle said.

"Easy for you say," said Willa. "But Sophie's mine. I can't bear to think of her being hurt. I won't give her up."

"What choice do you have?" Kyle said.

"Please, you can help find a place for her in America," Willa said. "A secret place. A private preserve. You know people."

"It's against everything I believe in," Kyle said. But he found it hard to meet Willa's eyes.

"Just this once—for old times' sake," Willa pleaded.

"Those days are over," Kyle said. "You know that. You made your decision when you went to work at a zoo."

"But I work for animals too, Kyle," Willa said.

"We've already had this argument," said Kyle. "As far as I'm concerned, it's finished."

Willa bit her lip, then blurted out, "She's pregnant, Kyle."

"What?" Kyle said.

"Sophie's pregnant," Willa repeated.

Kyle stared at her, then shook his head. "You are desperate, aren't you, Willa? But sorry, no sale. I'm not buying it."

"But it's true," she said.

"Say I believe you, which I don't," Kyle said. "What if Sophie was pregnant? The baby would live out its life in a cage too."

Willa opened her mouth to answer, but Kyle cut her off. "She doesn't belong to you, Willa. She's not your child. She should be with other gorillas, not selling tickets for a zoo."

"You won't help me?" Willa asked in a voice that showed she already knew the answer.

"No," Kyle said. "Now, why don't you go looking for another job? And let me get on with mine."

He saw Willa's head drop, her shoulders slump. He watched in silence as she went out the door. Then he went back to his desk and the pamphlet he was writing. He sat down in front of his word processor and punched the first key his eye fell on.

☠   ☠   ☠

An hour later Kyle was still at his desk. The computer screen still had only one meaningless letter on it. And Kyle still was seeing Willa's beaten look in his mind's eye.

It was as cruel a sight as any tormented animal he had ever seen. And he had seen many.

He tried to call them to mind. He wanted to be reminded of his life's work. But all he could see was Willa.

Willa as she was now, so hurt.

And Willa as he had known her years ago, when they had been so happy together.

He clicked off his machine and stood up.

He knew what he was going to do.

There was one thing he never had been able to endure, no matter what the reasons were.

A living creature in pain.

He picked up a bag of tools. He left the office. He got into his truck. And he drove to the zoo.

They were already saving money at the place. The lights were off. That was fine with Kyle. He had a flashlight to see by as he picked the lock on the gate.

If Willa ever smiled again, she'd smile at this joke, he thought. He had learned to break into places like this to fight people like her. Now she had to be thankful that he was so good at it.

He didn't need his flashlight as he moved

through the zoo grounds. He knew the layout like the back of his hand. He went to the building marked SICK ANIMAL. Willa might be there, staying close to Sophie till the end.

But Willa's camp bed was empty. So was Sophie's cage.

Kyle scribbled a short note to Willa. Just enough to tell her whom to contact tomorrow. He tucked it under her pillow. Then he headed for the warehouse.

He used his flashlight as he picked the lock, then snapped it off when the lock clicked open. The zoo still might have the money to pay for a watchman. But there was no sign of one as he entered the big darkened room, only the low murmur of animal noises.

Kyle gritted his teeth. He wanted to free every single creature boxed up in here—so badly that it hurt. But there was only so much he could do tonight.

His flashlight had an adjustable beam. He set it on low as he moved through the maze of stacked crates, examining their labels.

Suddenly he stopped and stared. Down a shadowy aisle was an open metal door.

Swiftly he moved to it.

It was the door of a large metal box. By the open door was a label:

GORLLA. NAME: SOPHIE. NO LONGER ZOO PROPERTY.

He shined his light inside.

It was empty except for the straw on the floor.

Kyle turned and whispered loudly, "Willa? Where are you? Don't worry. It's me, Kyle. I'm here to help."

Suddenly he sensed something behind him.

He whirled around—and was slammed off his feet.

His head was spinning, but he managed to get up.

Again he was hit by a sledgehammer blow. He went crashing into a stack of crates.

Dazed, he heard the howling of a wolf. He looked up to see the crate that caged the animal toppling off the top of the stack.

"No!" he screamed, throwing up his hands against the last hateful cage he would ever see.

Chapter FOURTEEN

"Is Willa still in there?" asked Scully.

She gestured toward the zoo's conference room. Inside, Willa was facing the police.

"She's still there," Mulder said. "Did you find anything in her hideaway?"

Scully had been checking out the room where Willa had kept Sophie.

"I found this in a desk drawer," Scully said. "I think you'll find it interesting."

She handed Mulder a newspaper clipping. It was yellowed with age.

"Interesting indeed," said Mulder. In the clipping were two photos. One showed Kyle Lang and Willa Ambrose smiling together for the camera. Both were much younger. The other showed a tiny gorilla. The headline read: COUPLE SAVES BABY GORILLA FROM SMUGGLERS Beneath it a smaller headline said: NATURALISTS WILLA AMBROSE AND KYLE LANG WILL BRING THE ANIMAL BACK TO U.S.

"So Willa and Kyle used to go together," Mulder said.

"And I can guess what drove them apart," said Scully. "Kyle must have wanted to turn Sophie loose. Willa wouldn't let her go."

"Makes sense," said Mulder. "A classic love triangle. Man, woman, and gorilla."

"Except that the story didn't end there," Scully said. She showed Mulder the note from Kyle she had found under Willa's pillow.

"It seems perhaps Sophie brought them back together again," Mulder said. "But only one person can tell us for sure."

"Right," Scully said. She opened the door to the conference room.

Willa sat in a chair. Her back was rigid and she was tight-lipped. Three sheriff's deputies stood around her. They looked tired. Willa was still stonewalling.

"I already told you, I heard the animals going crazy," she was saying. "I got up out of bed to check on Sophie. I saw she was gone. And then I found Kyle."

Scully joined the circle of lawmen. Mulder chose to stand by the wall. He liked to watch Scully when she got her teeth into a case.

Now she took over the questioning. "Do you know what Kyle was doing there?"

"No," Willa said.

"We have a witness who saw you visiting Kyle's office last night," Scully said. "Is that true?"

"Yes," Willa said.

"For what purpose?" Scully asked.

"To tell him he'd won," Willa said. "That the zoo was being shut down. That Sophie was being sent back to Africa."

"Did you ask him to help you?" Scully asked.

"Help me do what?" Willa said.

"Help you keep Sophie from being taken away," Scully said.

"No," answered Willa. "That would be against everything Kyle believed in."

Scully's voice turned hard. "But you asked him anyway."

Willa did not flinch. "No," she answered firmly.

"Then what was he doing in at the zoo last night?" Scully demanded. "And why did he leave you this note?" Scully pulled it out and read it aloud. " 'Willa, let's talk. Kyle.' "

Willa shrugged. "I have no idea."

"Did he visit the zoo often?" Scully asked.

"If he did, it was late at night—when he jumped the fence like a good W.A.O. soldier," Willa said. Then she added, "Why not ask Agent Mulder what happened here? His theory is even weirder than yours. He thinks it's an alien abduction."

All eyes turned to Mulder.

Mulder cleared his throat. "I think the questioning has touched all bases," he said. "Agent Scully, can I talk to you a minute—outside?"

Scully grimaced. She had no choice but to go

along with him. She could have used thumbscrews and Willa wouldn't have told her anything more.

Still, Scully felt hot under the collar. Outside, she turned to Mulder and said accusingly, "You think she's telling the truth. You actually believe that aliens stole Sophie and killed Kyle."

"Why do you say that?" Mulder said.

"Kyle's death and the animal's disappearance are exactly like what happened with the tiger," Scully said.

"Yes," Mulder said.

But Scully heard an unusual note in Mulder's voice.

A note of doubt.

"Don't tell me you're having second thoughts about aliens loose in the world," she said.

"Not about that," said Mulder. "But in the case of Sophie, something doesn't add up."

"What?" Scully asked.

"Willa's reactions," Mulder said, still sounding puzzled.

"Reactions to what?" asked Scully.

"To losing the animal she loved so much," Mulder said. "No way she could mask her grief so well. No way she could stay so cool."

"Which means?" said Scully.

"I think she knows where Sophie is," Mulder said. "And Kyle Lang died because he knew how far she would go to keep Sophie. He wanted to save her from risking everything. But he didn't succeed."

"So you think she killed him," Scully said.

"I think she'd do anything for that animal," Mulder said.

"Even wait on top of a stack of crates for her old boyfriend to walk underneath?" Scully shook her head.

"I'm not entirely sure of what happened last night," Mulder said. "I think a closer examination of the body will give us a clearer picture."

Scully nodded. "I'll get on it," she said.

"And I'll check out the warehouse again," Mulder said. "There might be something we overlooked."

"Okay," said Scully. "Keep the car here. I'll hitch a ride with the cops to the station. The morgue is right across the street."

Mulder watched her go, then headed for the warehouse. The door was open. Mulder walked among the stacks of crates. Only an occasional animal sound disturbed the silence. Most of the caged creatures must have been sleeping after the uproar of the night before.

He reached the metal box that had held the gorilla. Opening its door, he looked inside.

Nothing.

He closed the door and examined the concrete floor outside the cage.

Something.

A scattering of straw leading down the aisle to the door.

Not much. But enough to hint that the gorilla might have escaped that way—or been taken along that path by force.

Next Mulder's gaze traveled to where Kyle's corpse had been found. The crate that had killed him still lay on the ground as evidence. The wolf that had been in it was in another crate now, waiting to be shipped to California.

Mulder tried to imagine how the crate had fallen. He looked around carefully.

"Well, well," he murmured, seeing the cattle prod hanging on the wall. "So they found something for Ed Meecham to do to earn his pay. They had him keeping the animals in line."

Mulder stared at the prod with distaste—until a sound outside made him move swiftly to the door.

"Speak of the devil," he muttered as Ed Meecham let himself into the zoo garage.

By the time Meecham drove out of the garage in a zoo truck, Mulder was in his car, waiting.

He waited until the truck pulled into the street and then followed it.

It wasn't as good as tracking aliens. But it would have to do.

Chapter FIFTEEN

Mulder kept Ed Meecham's truck in sight as it drove down the highway toward the setting sun.

It was dark by the time Meecham stopped beside a large building in the middle of nowhere.

From its looks, it had once been a factory. But now it was abandoned. Meecham's headlights showed broken windows and grimy brick.

Mulder had kept his headlights off. From a distance he watched Meechham turn off his headlights and get out of his truck. Then Meecham turned on a flashlight, pulled out a pistol, and disappeared into the building.

Quickly Mulder followed. His own pistol was in his hand as he went through the open doorway.

Meecham moved down a hallway ahead of him.

"Put it down, Ed," Mulder said.

Startled, Meecham whirled around. He caught Mulder in his flashlight beam.

Mulder leveled his pistol and shook his head. "I think there's been enough violence already. Don't you?"

"I didn't kill Kyle Lang," Meecham said.

"Put down the gun and we'll talk about it," Mulder told him.

Meecham stared at Mulder's weapon. Then he dropped his.

Still holding his pistol on Meecham, Mulder picked up the abandoned weapon. It was a tranquilizer gun.

"I'm only doing what she paid me to do," Meecham said. "I needed the money. They weren't going to give me my pension. Said they were out of funds."

"My sympathy. I really feel for you," Mulder said dryly. Then he demanded, "Where's the animal?"

"Animal? What—?" Meecham started to say. Then he saw the look in Mulder's eyes and said, "Down the hall."

"Okay, you're going to show me," Mulder said. "We're going to go there together."

With a glance at Mulder's gun, Meecham nodded. He led the way down one hall, then another, his flashlight beam playing in front of him.

As they moved down the second hallway, Mulder heard a thumping, like the beating of a drum.

"What's that?" he asked.

"The gorilla," Meecham said. "She's throwing herself against the door. She's gone crazy."

The pounding grew louder. Meecham stopped in front of a thick metal door that shook each time the gorilla slammed against it.

"She's scared," Mulder said, grimacing. He could almost feel the impact each time she hit the door.

"Yeah, well, she's going to kill herself," said Meecham.

Mulder shuddered as Sophie hit the door full force again.

That made up his mind.

"Okay, Ed," Mulder said. "You're going to save her."

He held the tranquilizer gun out to Meecham.

"But—" Meecham began.

"I've heard you say how good you are with animals," Mulder said. "Now prove it."

His jaw tightening, Meecham took the gun.

"Give me the flashlight," Mulder said. "I'll shine it on her.

Slowly, cautiously, Meecham opened the door, his body rigid with fear. He moved as if he were walking barefoot on glass. Mulder was right behind him, flashlight in one hand, pistol in the other.

The flashlight showed that Sophie had retreated from the door. She was somewhere in the pitch black of the room.

"I got one shot with this thing," Meecham said. "You be ready with your pistol, hear?"

"Where is she?" Mulder asked.

"I think in the far corner," Meecham said.

Mulder swung the flashlight beam in that direction.

Suddenly the flashlight flew from his hand as he was knocked onto his back.

He caught a glimpse of Sophie's angry face before she smashed into him.

Her musky odor filled his nostrils as he heard the pop of the tranquilizer gun. His hand tightened on his own weapon.

Then the gorilla was gone. She had fled back into the dark. The room was black again, except for a bar of light on the floor from the fallen flashlight.

"Ed?" Mulder said, sitting up. There was no answer.

"Ed!" Mulder shouted. "Hey!"

He heard Meecham's muffled voice. "I missed the shot."

Meecham was on the other side of the door. Mulder tried to open it. It was locked.

"Open the door, Ed!" Mulder screamed.

"You've got a gun. Use it," muttered Meecham.

"Ed, listen," Mulder pleaded.

There was no answer. Meecham was gone.

Mulder turned back to peer into the darkness.

He longed to pick up the flashlight. But he did not want to cross the space between him and it. It would leave him exposed to sudden attack.

He could only pray that Sophie could understand him.

He could only hope she would believe him.

"Sophie," he said. "I'm your friend. I want to help you. I want to help your baby."

From the darkness came a low growling. Mulder could hear the anger and desperation in it.

Sophie had been betrayed once too often. She had stopped trusting human beings.

Mulder couldn't blame her.

Nor could he blame her for wanting to do anything that might save her baby.

His pistol felt heavy in his hand. It seemed to weigh more with every passing second.

He had never hesitated to use it on the guilty when he had to. But to use it on the innocent was a far different thing.

The situation was easy enough to see.

It was kill or be killed.

He desperately wished that making the choice was that easy.

But he had run out of time to make up his mind.

Sophie roared three times. Then she charged.

Chapter SIXTEEN

Pain slashed across Mulder's forehead.

Sophie's nails had raked his skin.

The light from the flashlight on the floor turned from white to bloodred in his eyes.

In that red haze he saw Sophie standing huge above him as he crouched on all fours.

She was raising her arm for another brutal blow.

Mulder raised his pistol. His finger tensed on the trigger.

But he could not make himself pull it. The gun barrel wavered as his arm trembled. Inside him a terrible tug-of-war was taking place.

Kill or be killed?

Mulder could never be sure what he would have done if Sophie hadn't suddenly frozen.

She turned and ran back into the dark. Mulder looked around to see what had frightened her.

He blinked as glowing vapor poured into the room.

In the misty light Sophie began to melt away before him.

He saw her eyes giving him a helpless farewell. He saw her hands making three last signs.

That was all he saw as white light exploded—and he plunged again into blackness.

"Mulder. . . . Mulder. . . ."

From what seemed miles away came Scully's worried voice.

Mulder's eyelids felt as if they were made of stone, but he forced them open. Early-morning light filled the room. Scully was looking down at him.

"Mulder, lie still," she told him. She turned and said to one of the two policemen behind her, "Radio for a paramedic."

"I'm okay," Mulder told her as he sat up on the floor. He shook his head to clear it. He looked around the room. Sophie was gone.

"Where is she?" he asked.

"Where is who?" Scully said.

"Sophie—they took her," Mulder said.

"Lie back, Mulder, you're still in shock," Scully said.

Instead, Mulder got to his feet. "Meecham—" he said.

"Ed Meecham's been arrested," Scully said. "He was picked up heading for the state line. He told us you were here."

"Where's Willa?" asked Mulder.

"Outside in a squad car," Scully said. "I examined Kyle and found evidence that he had died a wrongful death. Seems he'd been beaten with a cattle prod. I went to confront Willa with the news just as she was getting ready to clear out. It took almost no pressure to make her fold. She confessed to hiring Ed. She said he was keeping Sophie in a building somewhere on this highway." Scully shook her head sadly. "The threat of losing Sophie really made her flip."

"I've got to talk with her," Mulder said.

"Mulder. You're in no condition to—"

But he was already on his way.

He found Willa in the backseat of the squad car. She was staring dead ahead with empty eyes.

But when she saw Mulder, she came to life. "Where's Sophie?" she demanded.

"She's gone," Mulder said.

Pain twisted Willa's face. Then she glared at him with hatred.

"What did Ed do to her?" she said. "I was a fool to turn to him for help. But he was the only one left."

"It wasn't Ed," Mulder said.

"This is a nightmare," Willa said, her whole body shaking. "None of this should have happened. Ed panicked when he saw Kyle. Kyle wasn't supposed to be there." She ran a hand through her hair in despair. "He's gone. Sophie's gone. I've lost everything." She buried her face in her hands.

"Ms. Ambrose, listen to me," Mulder pleaded. "I need your help. Sophie tried to tell me something."

Willa looked up the moment she heard Sophie's name. "What?" she asked.

"What does this mean?" Mulder asked. He imitated the signs Sophie had made before the white light had swallowed her.

"It doesn't make sense," Willa said.

"What does it mean?" Mulder asked again.

"Man save man," Willa said.

She and Mulder stared at each other, both trying to understand the three words.

They did not get far. A voice spoke through static on the squad car's radio. "All vehicles in the vicinity: a large animal reported running wild. Last sighted on the interstate just west of the service road off Ninety-second Avenue."

"It's her," said Mulder.

"She's trying to get back to the zoo," said Willa.

"Maybe," said Mulder.

He caught sight of Scully and the cops coming out of the building. He shouted the news to them.

The cops jumped into the front seat. Scully got in back with Mulder and Willa. The car took off.

"Hurry, would you!" Willa almost screamed at the cop who was driving.

Half an hour later the car pulled up to a group of other squad cars parked at the side of a country road. Near them was an overturned civilian car. The scene was bathed in chill silver light under a gray morning sky.

As soon as the squad car stopped, Willa was out of it like a shot.

Mulder and Scully were right behind her.

Willa ran up to the first cop she saw. "Where is she?" Willa demanded.

"She?" asked the cop.

"Sophie," Willa said.

"Sophie?"

"The runaway gorilla," Mulder explained.

"Why didn't you say so?" the cop said. "Over there."

He pointed toward a small clump of trees that stood lonely on the bare horizon.

Willa broke into a run. Mulder and Scully followed.

When they reached the trees they found more police.

"What happened here, Officer?" Scully asked one of them.

The cop said, "Animal ran across the road, got hit by a car. Car got totaled when it went off the road trying to avoid impact. The driver's okay, though."

"And the animal?" Willa asked, barely able to get the words out.

"It tried to keep on going," said the cop. "It made it this far."

He pointed toward some undergrowth. Two cops were standing there, looking at the ground.

Willa shoved herself between them. She knelt down by the animal that lay there in a heap.

"Oh no. No, no, no, no," Willa moaned as she stroked the gorilla's face. She leaned forward and spoke into the animal's ear, as if trying to wake her. "Sophie . . . Sophie . . ."

The cop nearest her shook his head. "She's dead, ma'am," he said.

Willa looked up and said, "Please, tell me one thing. Which way was she running?"

The cop looked bewildered. "Sorry, but—"

"Which way was she running—toward the zoo or away from it?" Willa asked.

The cop lifted his shoulders. "Sorry, I don't know, ma'am," he said.

Mulder stood beside Scully, watching helplessly as Willa collapsed in grief on top of the corpse. He couldn't give her the answer she wanted. He had questions of his own.

All he could do was stare at the animal's right hand, so very much like a human's.

The fingers were frozen in a sign that Mulder recognized. The sign he had seen Willa use so long ago.

I love you.

Chapter SEVENTEEN

The next morning Mulder and Scully drove their rental car back to the airport.

They drove in silence. There didn't seem to be much to talk about.

This case was finished.

The courts would decide what would happen to Willa.

The city council would decide what would happen to the zoo.

And nobody could tell what would happen to the animals now being shipped all over the country.

"You know, it's strange what I keep remembering," Scully said out of the blue.

"What's that?" said Mulder.

"I keep remembering that deserted shopping plaza, after the tiger cleared it," Scully said. "It looked so spooky. It was like a world from which all life had fled. There were only empty buildings left. Funny, huh?"

"Funny," agreed Mulder.

Then he said, "I might as well finish taping my observations. You'll need them for your report to the brass."

He picked up the mike of his tape recorder.

"The crimes committed in Fairfield were the acts of desperate people who were doing more than fighting one another. They were fighting a force none of them could have imagined, much less defeated. A force whose purpose is beyond our sure knowledge. Could aliens be trying to protect animals that we are driving toward extinction? Is it a judgment that we cannot protect them ourselves? Is it a reflection of the fact that the rate of exinction has risen a thousand times above normal in this century? Could we humans soon find ourselves alone on this planet and facing extinction ourselves? Might our survival and the survival of all other living things on earth depend on aliens who may be stocking their own zoos? Or, in the last words of a creature that could not survive, will man save man?"

Mulder put down his mike.

"I guess that sums it up, Scully," he said.

"I'm afraid it does," she answered, keeping her eyes on the road.

"So many questions, so few answers." Mulder looked out the car window at a world that offered no answers at all.

Except perhaps for the billboard he read as they drove by.

On it in three-foot letters was a quotation from the Bible:

"A man has no preeminence above a beast; for all is vanity."

LES MARTIN has written dozens of books for young readers, including RAIDERS OF THE LOST ARK and INDIANA JONES AND THE TEMPLE OF DOOM movie storybooks, and many Young Indiana Jones middle-grade novels. He has also adapted many classic works of fiction for young readers including THE LAST OF THE MOHICANS, EDGAR ALLAN POE'S TALES OF TERROR, and THE VAMPIRE. Mr. Martin is a resident of New York City.